The Boy Who Ate Dog Biscuits

By Betsy Sachs

illustrated by Margot Apple

cover illustrated by Bonnie Leick

A STEPPING STONE BOOK™

Random House 🏠 New York

Text copyright © 1989 by Betsy Sachs. Illustrations copyright © 1989 by
Margot Apple. Cover illustration copyright © 2005 by Bonnie Leick.
Published in the United States by Random House Children's
Books, a division of Random House, Inc., New York, and simultaneously
in Canada by Random House of Canada Limited, Toronto.

www.randomhouse.com/kids

Library of Congress Cataloging-in-Publication Data
Sachs, Elizabeth-Ann.
The boy who ate dog biscuits / by Elizabeth Sachs ; illustrated by Margot Apple
   p.   cm.
"A Stepping Stone book."
SUMMARY: All Billy wants is a dog of his own, but he gets a baby sister instead.
ISBN 0-394-84778-4 (pbk.) — ISBN 0-394-94778-9 (lib. bdg.)
[1. Babies—Fiction. 2. Brothers and sisters—Fiction.]   I. Apple, Margot, ill.
II. Title.   PZ7.S1186Bo 1989 [E]—dc19 89-3905

Printed in the United States of America   27 26 25 24 23 22 21

To Carl, my favorite brother!

1

"Billy! Don't forget your bed."

"Mom!" Billy Getten called back to his mother. "Cleaning my room doesn't make sense. It only gets messy again."

Billy pulled his torn pants from under the bed. Where would he hide them? He didn't want his mother to find out he'd ruined his new clothes.

A yellow dog biscuit fell out of the pants pocket. It was covered with lint. Bright green clay was stuck to one end.

Billy picked the fuzzy lint off and most of the clay. He took a small bite. Chicken flavor was his favorite.

Billy took another bite. Then he put the

other half in his hip pocket. He wanted to save some for later.

He dug his schoolbag out of the closet and stuffed the torn pants into it. His mother would never think of looking there now that it was summer.

"Mom!" Billy called. He straightened up his bed. "I'm done."

Billy pulled on a faded blue T-shirt and brushed back his straight brown hair. He grabbed his baseball cap from the top of the dresser. In the mirror he made sure the cap was on backward.

"Looks better," Billy's mother said from the doorway.

Billy shut his closet door quickly. "Can I go out now?"

"I want you to come hold Sarah while I make her bed."

"Do I have to?"

"Of course."

"But Howard's waiting."

"Tell him to come in, then."

"And see me holding a baby!"

"I'm sure he holds his brother."

No way, Billy thought. Howard would never.

Billy turned to the window. "Five minutes," he shouted.

"Billy, please!" Mrs. Getten picked up a pile of clothing off the floor.

"Okay," he said. "I'm coming."

He followed his mother down the hall. The baby's room was white, with little pink flowers all over the walls. In the crib his baby sister was playing with a red plastic ring.

"Sit in the rocker," Mrs. Getten said. Then she put Sarah in Billy's lap.

Billy looked at his sister. She had dark red hair just like his mother's, but her face was all bunched up. "I thought babies were supposed to be cute. How come she looks like an old monkey?"

"She is cute," Mrs. Getten said. "She looks like Grandpa Stewie."

Billy's mother shook out the clean pink sheets. She began to make up the crib.

"Goo, goo," said Sarah. She snuggled against Billy's chest.

"She doesn't do anything," Billy said, "but sleep and poop."

"Ha!" said his mother. "Come feed her
sometime."

"That's boring too."

"Hardly."

"I can't do stuff with her like I could with a dog. You know I've been praying for a dog for a long time. Even before Sarah was born!"

Billy's mother said, "Sometimes it takes a while for prayers to be answered. And it doesn't always happen the way you expect."

Billy wasn't sure what his mother meant. All he knew was that he prayed for a dog, but a baby came instead.

Mrs. Getten put Sarah back in her crib. "Nana and Grandpa won't find anything strange in your room when they stay over, will they?"

"No, Mom. Can I go out now?" Billy inched toward the bedroom door.

"Well, all right. Just don't let the screen door slam." Mrs. Getten eased the crib bars up on Sarah's bed. "I think she's finally going to take a nap."

Billy didn't really hear his mother. He was already heading for the stairs.

He crashed through the kitchen. He jumped from the top of the porch. The screen door slammed, but Billy didn't notice. He was already down the driveway.

2

Howard Rosa sat on the stone wall at the end of Billy's driveway. The backs of his red high tops banged against the wall. His laces were untied. "What took you so long?" he asked.

"Nothing."

"What do you mean, nothing? I've been waiting all morning." Howard's mother let him spike his hair. He peered at Billy through yellow sunglasses.

Billy could see himself in the lenses. "My grandparents are coming for my birthday. I had to pick up my room."

Howard shook his head. "Bor-ing."

"Tell me about it. My birthday isn't till next Sunday. And I *still* had to clean." Billy sat down on the stone wall. "Did you get the thing?"

Howard pulled a small black box out of his back pocket. It was an electric garage-door opener from his house.

Howard smiled at Billy. Billy smiled back.

"Let's go to my house." Howard slid off the wall.

They cut through a neighbor's side yard over to the next street. None of the other kids were around. It was very quiet.

"So what do you want to do with it?" Billy kicked a stone ahead of him as he walked.

"See how far away from the garage I can get and still make it go."

They hid behind the bushes across the street from Howard's house. Howard pushed the button on the black box.

At the top of the Rosas' driveway, the garage door groaned and shook. Slowly it lifted and stayed up.

"Aw-right!" Howard punched Billy's arm.

"Ouch." Billy rubbed his skin. He hated when Howard did that.

"Now, listen," said Howard. "I'm going down

to the Breens' house. You stand on the side-walk and signal with your arms. Okay?"

"When do I get to do it?"

"It's mine. I go first." Howard stood up. He straightened his sunglasses.

"Boy," Billy muttered. He watched as Howard ran down the block as far as Chrissy Breen's house. Chrissy was going into third grade with Billy and Howard.

The garage door rattled down and up and then down again. Billy raised his arms as a signal to Howard.

Howard ran toward a mailbox that was five houses away.

The garage door rattled up and down. Billy signaled again.

When Howard was nine houses away, Howard's little brother, Frankie, came tod-dling across the driveway. He was on his way to the sandbox under the trees. The door went up. Frankie dropped his doll and stood watching.

Howard came running back. "Hey!" he shouted. "You're supposed to signal, dummy!"

Billy pointed toward the driveway. "Do it

again and watch your brother."

Howard pressed the garage-door opener. The door went up. Frankie's head went up.

Then the door came down. Frankie's head did too.

Billy and Howard started laughing. They stopped when they saw Frankie step on the bottom handle of the garage door and grab the lock. They ran up the driveway.

"Ride me," said Frankie. He gave Howard and Billy a grape-jelly smile.

"Oh, wow!" Howard whooped. "Let's see if he can ride it. Hang on, Frankie!"

Billy wondered if it was a good idea. He didn't say anything, though. Howard would call him a baby.

"Ride me," Frankie giggled. "Ride, ride, ride!"

Howard danced around, shouting, "Count down! Ten, nine, eight—"

Just then the side door of his house opened. Howard's mother came out. "What in the world is going on out here?" she asked.

"Nothing." Howard tried to hide the electric opener behind his back.

Frankie clung to the door handle. "Ride me!" he shouted. "Up, down! Up, down!"

"Howard! Are you crazy?" Mrs. Rosa picked Frankie up.

Frankie kicked his legs against his mother's side. His arms flapped in the air. "Up, down!" he screamed.

"All right. Let's have it." Mrs. Rosa took the opener. She pressed the button. The door groaned. It shook. It did not go up. "Well, that's just dandy," she said. "In the house, Howard Rosa. You'll have to go home, Billy."

"Ride, Mama!" Frankie cried. His face was all red. "Ride, Mama, ride!" he wailed as she carried him into the house.

3

"Inside, Billy." Mr. Getten stood in the kitchen doorway. He was wearing overalls. There were little curls of wood in his dark hair.

"Do I have to?" Billy asked.

Mr. Getten frowned.

"But it's not even lunchtime yet."

Mr. Getten didn't say a word. Billy got the message. He walked past his father into the cool, dark kitchen.

Billy's mother was sitting at the kitchen table. She looked angry too. Billy knew it was going to be a terrible afternoon.

"Sit," said his father.

Billy slid into a wooden chair. He looked

from his mother to his father. No one said anything. The silence felt scary.

"How could you do such a stupid thing?" Mrs. Getten finally said.

"What?" Billy tried to play dumb.

"You know what." Mr. Getten's chair scraped on the floor as he pulled closer to the table.

"Mrs. Rosa just called," his mother said. "So we know what you were up to."

"Oh." Billy felt for the dog biscuit in his pocket. He fingered it.

"This is serious," Mrs. Getten said. "Frankie could have been hurt."

"It was his idea."

"What do you mean?" asked Mr. Getten.

"We didn't tell him to get on. He just did."

"Frankie's a baby," Mr. Getten said. "He doesn't know any better."

Billy snapped the biscuit in half inside his pocket.

"Suppose Frankie had been hurt." His mother shook her head. "It was very irresponsible of you two."

Billy didn't know what "irresponsible" meant. It didn't sound like a fun word.

He leaned under the table, pretending to tie a shoelace. He popped the piece of biscuit into his mouth.

"Sit up, Billy," Mrs. Getten snapped. "And stop fooling around."

Billy held the dry biscuit under his tongue.

"The door's broken," said Mrs. Getten. "You'll have to help pay for fixing it."

"What!" Billy coughed.

"I think you should give your allowance to Mrs. Rosa," said Mr. Getten.

"My allowance!" Billy choked as he swallowed.

"You have to learn responsibility, young man!"

"Boy, I get punished and it wasn't even my idea."

"Howard told his mother it was."

"That rat!"

"Either way. You should have told Howard no."

"Da-ad! He'd think I was a big baby."

"Sometimes you have to be different from your friends."

Billy put his elbows on the table. "But I need my allowance to buy dog biscuits."

"You shouldn't be eating those things anyway."

Billy put his head on his arm. "Sarah's doctor even said they're okay."

"He also said not too many." Mrs. Getten frowned. "They're meant for dogs. Not people."

"But how can I teach Dr. Mike's dogs any tricks if I don't have biscuits?"

"You should have thought of that first," his father said.

"Are you sure Dr. Mike doesn't mind you playing over there?" asked Mrs. Getten.

"It's okay. I checked," Billy said. "Honest."

"You'd better shape up, young man."

Billy looked from one parent to the other. "If you'd just get me a dog for my birthday, I'd be real good."

Mrs. Getten shook her head. "I think you should be good first."

"You don't seem like you're ready for a dog, son."

"Not ready? That's all I ever wanted!"

His mother stood.

His father said, "If you'd help around here, maybe we'd consider a dog. But not with the kind of stunt you pulled this morning."

Billy didn't dare say what he was thinking. They really should have gotten a dog instead of a baby. What good was a baby? She couldn't even run after a stick.

4

Billy used the shortcut through the empty lot to the next street. He stood at the corner and waited for the light to change.

How could he teach Dr. Mike's dogs tricks without dog biscuits? Dr. Mike probably wouldn't want him to come over without them.

The traffic on the street went by slowly. Finally it was safe for him to cross.

By the time he turned the next corner, Billy could hear yelping and barking out in the yard. The sounds made him feel better.

He cut across the grass and ran the rest of the way up to the blue house. It had a fence all the way around the backyard.

The sign on the lawn said: DR. MICHAELS, VETERINARIAN. Billy sounded the word out. "Vet-er-i-nar-i-an." He liked the word. It was a pretty word, and a big one. To Billy it meant someone who liked to take care of dogs as much as he did.

Billy went through the metal gate. It clanged shut. Dogs of all sizes and shapes ran over to him.

"Hi, girl." A fat tan puppy licked Billy's hand. Her tongue was pink and warm.

"Hey, fella. Want your belly rubbed?" Billy scratched a spotted mutt's stomach.

A small brown poodle danced around Billy's feet. He nipped playfully at Billy's laces. "What are you doing, Killer?" He patted the poodle's head.

"Hel-lo, Billy," a voice called through an open door.

"Hi, Dr. Mike."

Dr. Mike came into the yard. She was short and blond and wore a blue lab coat. "Am I ever glad to see you," she said. "A policeman just brought in another stray dog."

Billy followed her into the animal hospital. They walked down a long hall lined with big green cages. There was a dog in every one.

The room at the end of the hall had more cages. Some were empty, and others had kittens or puppies in them.

Dr. Mike opened a cage. She lifted out a big gray cat. "Want to hold this guy?"

"Sure." Billy took the cat in his arms. "Hi there, fella."

The cat whined and squirmed. Billy rubbed his face in the cat's thick gray hair. "It's okay," he whispered.

"He's just a little nervous." Dr. Mike moved toward the operating room.

Billy followed. "What's wrong with him?"

"He needs a tooth taken out." Dr. Mike sprayed the stainless-steel table with cleaner. Then she wiped it with a paper towel. "Okay, you can put him down."

Billy petted the cat. Dr. Mike got ready to give him a shot. "Billy," she said, "grab the scruff of his neck. Shake his head gently. That'll distract him."

Billy liked helping Dr. Mike. He always learned a lot about animals.

He watched her give the shot. "Can I stay?" he asked.

Dr. Mike smiled. "No. I really need you to run the dogs out in the back field."

Billy wanted to tell Dr. Mike about the dog biscuits, but he didn't. He could see she was busy. "Okay, I'll be outside."

"I'll call you when I'm done."

Billy hurried down the hall. The best part of summer was being at Dr. Mike's. Everyone in town knew she cared about animals. The police and firemen brought her stray dogs and cats. She always tried to find out who owned the animals or to find them new owners. Often she kept the ones nobody would adopt.

Today Billy counted six stray dogs out in the back. He petted the big black mutt who was blind. Lola had been at Dr. Mike's the longest. She sniffed his hand. Then she licked it.

Billy dropped on the grass and rolled onto his back. The mutt with no tail jumped on

Billy's stomach and washed his face with a long, warm tongue. "Quit it!" Billy laughed. The dog kept right on licking.

After that Billy wrestled a terrier. When the dog was tired, she played dead. "Good doggie," Billy said. "You remembered your trick from last time." He slipped her a piece of his only biscuit.

Next Billy played fetch with the two brown puppies. He loved to fool them by pretending to throw the stick across the yard. They would go bounding over the field trying to find it. Then they would give up and come running back.

"Got you." Billy pretended to throw the stick again. They went chasing off across the grass.

When Billy saw Dr. Mike standing in the doorway, he crossed the field. He always did exactly what she said. Billy wanted to keep coming back.

"Where's Howard today?" she asked as Billy came in.

Billy shrugged his shoulders. Howard's name made him feel bad again.

"Something wrong?"

"I won't be able to bring treats anymore."

"Oh?"

"I lost my allowance."

"That's too bad."

"Yeah, me and Howard got in trouble."

"I see," she said.

"We were playing with the Rosas' garage opener. Mrs. Rosa didn't like us giving Howard's baby brother rides on the garage door."

Dr. Mike put a hand over her mouth. She made a funny noise. Was she laughing? Billy wasn't sure.

"Did it break?"

"Yeah. And I have to help pay with my allowance. So I won't have money for treats."

"I see," she said. "Well, I'll tell you what. You come every day, and I'll get the dog biscuits."

"Oh, wow!"

"Maybe I could even pay you. But I'd have to check with your parents."

"Ah." Billy frowned. "They're kinda mad at me. Don't call right now, okay?"

"Okay," she said.

Billy smiled. He wanted to be a vet just like Dr. Mike.

"It helps me a lot if you run the strays. I have so much to do with the regular dogs. I don't have much time for the strays."

Dr. Mike stopped in front of a cage. Inside was a stocky dog with short white hair and a stumpy tail. He had a brown-and-black patch around one eye. "Here's the stray the police found. I have to check him over before he can mix with the other dogs. I'm sure someone will claim him. He's no mutt."

"He's beautiful." Billy dug in his pocket for the last little piece of biscuit.

"Don't," said Dr. Mike. "Not until I'm sure he's okay."

The dog wagged his tail. He barked at Billy.

"Out you go now," said Dr. Mike. "I'll have the treats tomorrow."

5

When Billy got home, his grandparents' van was parked in the driveway.

"Well, hello there, darling!" his grandmother called from the porch. She was holding the baby in her lap.

Sarah had yellow food all over her face. There was some in her hair, too.

"Hiya, Nana." Billy came up the steps.

His grandfather pushed the screen door open with his cane. "We've been waiting for you," he called. He had on his cowboy hat.

"Hi, Grandpa."

"Come give me a kiss, Billy," his grandmother said.

Billy leaned over his grandmother. He kissed her on the cheek. She smelled funny. He backed away.

No, Billy thought, Nana didn't smell bad. It was Sarah. Yucky babies!

"What about me?" said Grandpa Stewie.

Billy grabbed his grandfather around the waist and squeezed hard. Grandpa Stewie whispered, "I have a big favor to ask you."

Billy looked up. He waited, but Grandpa Stewie just winked.

"It's time for supper," his mother yelled from the kitchen. "Go wash up, Billy."

Billy went into the downstairs bathroom and turned on the water. His hands smelled like dogs. It was a good smell. Billy decided not to use soap. Maybe then the smell would stay.

He dangled his fingers under the water. Little rivers of dirt ran down the sink. He shook his hands to dry them.

What did his grandfather want him to do? Last time he visited, Billy kept him company while he smoked cigars in the backyard. Billy's mother wouldn't let Grandpa Stewie smoke in the house.

"Billy." His grandfather rapped on the door. "Did you fall in?"

Billy laughed. He pictured a little person swimming in circles in the toilet. "Glub, glub, glub!" he yelled, and opened the door.

Grandpa Stewie leaned on his cane. "Billy," he said. "Will you go get the paper for me at the general store while we're here?"

"I'm not allowed to cross the highway by myself."

"If I drive, would you run into the store?"

"Sure."

"Thanks."

"Is that the favor?"

"Yes."

"That's easy," Billy said. He wondered why his grandpa had made a big deal over such a little thing.

6

Billy's grandparents stayed a whole week. Every day Billy and Grandpa Stewie went out for the paper.

On Saturday it was cool and breezy. Grandpa Stewie rolled down the windows in the van. As they were driving along, he said, "You're doing a good job, you know."

"I am?"

"Sure! Getting the paper for me like this each day."

"It's no big deal. It only takes a second to run in."

All of a sudden Billy thought Grandpa Stewie looked sad. Billy didn't know what to do. Finally he asked, "What's the matter, Grandpa?"

The old man shook his head. In a low voice he said, "I don't like talking about this. Sometimes my legs hurt so much, they don't want to walk me around. Not even to get the paper."

This time Billy kept quiet. He really didn't know what to say. He felt bad for his grandfather.

"Your getting the paper really helps me. From now on I want you to keep the change as pay."

"But I could just do it. For free. I like doing stuff with you."

"You don't hate money, do you?"

"No. I like it." Billy laughed.

"So keep the change, then."

"All right." Then Billy thought of something funny. "Now I get paid in money from you and in dog biscuits from Dr. Mike."

"That sounds fine."

"Could we stop at Dr. Mike's? We go right by."

"Just point the way."

Grandpa Stewie pulled into Dr. Mike's parking lot. He turned off the engine. Billy jumped out. "Hey, wait for me," Grandpa Stewie called after Billy. "My legs feel like walking today."

Billy watched Grandpa Stewie make his way up the path. His grandfather did walk slowly, as if his legs really hurt. Billy led him around to the side of the house where the dogs were fenced in. Grandpa Stewie sat down on a bench in the sun.

"Dr. Mike?" Billy called through the screen door. The hall was dark inside. He couldn't see anything. "Are you in there?"

Billy heard footsteps coming. Then Dr. Mike called, "Good morning." She was carrying a box of dog treats.

"Hi," Billy said as she stepped outside. "My grandfather's here."

"How do you do?" Dr. Mike put the box on the ground. She extended her hand. Grandpa Stewie used his cane to push himself up. "Oh, don't get up." She sat beside him. "Billy tells me you're visiting."

"For his birthday."

"Billy!" She turned to him. "I didn't know it was your birthday."

"Yeah. Tomorrow."

Dr. Mike smiled at him. To his grandfather she said, "Has Billy told you how much he's been helping me?"

Billy didn't want to stand around while they talked about him. It made him feel funny. He

grabbed the box of dog treats and began to fill his pockets with them. "I'm going to take care of the dogs now," he said.

The new white stray was out in the yard with the other dogs. He jumped against the fence when Billy opened the gate.

"Hey, there." The stray licked Billy's hand. "How you doing, doggie?"

The stray waited while Billy splashed water into the bowls. Then he trotted along with Billy.

"Are you dogging me, dog?" Billy laughed. He made it across the field without spilling any water.

The other dogs gathered around Billy. They whined and begged for treats. The white stray sat quietly. He kept his eyes on Billy.

"Here, fella." Billy tossed him a biscuit. Only then did he stop watching Billy and begin to chew.

When Billy moved away, the white stray followed him again. Billy leaned against a tree and watched the other dogs settle down for their morning snooze. The stray leaned against Billy's leg.

Billy looked down at him. He was such a great dog. "Listen," he whispered. "I know someone must own you. But I really want to take you home."

The stray barked. He put a paw on Billy's leg. "Shush," said Billy. "Not so loud. I don't want the other dogs to know."

The stray whimpered. He barked again softly.

Billy broke a biscuit in two. He and the dog each ate half of a chicken-cheese-flavored treat.

"You need a name," he said. "Something that really goes with you."

The stray seemed to understand what Billy was saying. He wagged his tail.

Grandpa Stewie tooted the horn. The stray followed Billy back to the gate.

Dr. Mike came out as Billy was leaving. "See you tomorrow. Say so long to your grandfather."

"Yup." Billy started down the walk. Then he turned around. "Dr. Mike, has anyone called about the new stray?"

She shook her head. "I'm pretty sure someone will, though. He's an expensive dog."

"I hope they don't."

"Remember our rule: Don't get too attached. He might be gone tomorrow."

"I know." Billy sighed.

"Let's just see what happens, okay?"

"Okay." Billy took a long look at the stray and slipped him one last biscuit through the fence.

7

That afternoon Billy sat on the kitchen steps. The sun beat down. The heat made it hard to think about a good dog name.

Through the open door he could hear his mother in the kitchen. She was talking to his grandfather. "Are you sure you can manage, Dad?"

"Yes, yes, of course," he said. "Have a good time at the mall."

"Sarah should sleep until we get back. I don't think you'll have any problems."

Mrs. Getten came outside. "Help Grandpa if he needs it, Billy." She started down the walk.

"Okay."

Mrs. Getten turned around. "I mean it, Billy. Don't just disappear."

"I won't."

Billy stood up so his grandmother could pass by him. "See you later, darling," she said.

Grandpa Stewie came out and sat on the porch. The crickets chirped in the grass.

Billy could hear laughing and screaming. The little kids next door were playing under the sprinkler.

"Cat got your tongue?" asked Grandpa Stewie.

"What?"

"That means you seem quiet."

"Oh," Billy said. "I wish the new dog at Dr. Mike's was mine."

"He does seem to have taken a shine to you."

"Yeah."

"Well, start saving your money, if you want a dog."

"You mean like for food and stuff?"

"Shots, leashes. Dogs are expensive."

"You think if I had lots of money, Mom and Dad would let me have a dog?"

"Money is only part of it."

"What else?"

"You have to take care of a dog. All the time, every day. Like you would a baby."

"I take care of dogs every day."

"That's true." Grandpa Stewie nodded. "Do your parents know how responsible you are about going to Dr. Mike's?"

"That's being responsible?"

"Sure."

"But I'm having fun."

"You're allowed to."

"I didn't know that."

"You should let your folks know."

"They'd never believe me."

"You have to speak up, my boy. Let people know what you're doing."

Billy wasn't sure he could do what his grandfather said. There was something else he needed to know. "You think if Dr. Mike gave me a job, I could buy that dog?"

"You don't need a job. I bet your parents would get you a dog if you'd just help out."

"You mean like if I cleaned my room? The boring stuff?"

"Might be boring, but it would show your parents you're willing to help. Like you do at Dr. Mike's."

"But cleaning's no fun."

"Being responsible isn't terrible all the time or fun all the time."

"Oh," said Billy.

"Give it a whirl. What have you got to lose?"

"Nothing," said Billy. "Except my dirty bedroom."

Inside the house Sarah started to cry.

"Uh-oh," Grandpa said. "She's not supposed to do that."

"My mom lets her cry sometimes." Sarah's wailing got louder.

"I don't know. That doesn't sound good to me."

"She might have pooped in her diaper."

"Do you know how to change her?"

Billy made a face. "Yuck."

"Well, let's go see."

Billy took the stairs two at a time. He opened the baby's bedroom door and peeked in. Sarah's face was red. There were tears on her cheeks. Her damp red hair was stuck to her head.

"Hey, Sarah." She stopped crying the minute she saw Billy.

"It doesn't smell bad in here," Billy said over his shoulder. "So I guess she didn't."

Grandpa Stewie took a deep breath and leaned on the doorknob. "Good thing. I was leaving town if she did."

Billy smiled. So he wasn't the only one who hated dirty diapers.

Sarah held up both hands. She looked at Billy. She made a sound like "Ah. Ah."

"What does she want?" asked Grandpa Stewie.

"That's her way of saying she wants to get up."

"Can you carry her?"

"Yeah. I'm allowed."

"Let's bring her downstairs."

Billy dropped the bars on the crib. He picked up Sarah. She weighed about the same as a good-size puppy.

Grandpa Stewie started down the hall. Billy and Sarah followed. "I'm glad you're here," Grandpa said. "I hate to admit it, but I could never have managed the stairs and a squirmy baby all by myself."

Billy didn't know what to say. His grandfather's words made him feel really good. Maybe being responsible wasn't so terrible after all.

8

Billy and Sarah followed Grandpa Stewie into the kitchen.

"Maybe she's hungry," Billy said. He strapped Sarah into her high chair.

Grandpa Stewie opened the refrigerator. "Think she'd like a beer?"

"Grandpa!" Billy laughed. "She can't have that!"

"Oh, I know."

Billy stood beside his grandfather. "See that little jar with green stuff? That's hers."

Billy got a spoon and put the baby food in a bowl. He sat in front of Sarah's high chair, like his mother did.

He put some mashed pea on the spoon. He tried to put some in Sarah's mouth.

She made a face. "Poo. Poo."

"No," said Billy. "Not poo-poo. Food, Sarah. *Food.*"

"Poo. Poo," said Sarah.

"Open wide," Grandpa Stewie said. He opened his mouth and wagged his tongue at her.

"Ahh," Billy said with his mouth wide open too.

Sarah smiled. She opened her mouth.

Billy put the spoon in her mouth. "That was easy."

Sarah made a face. She spit pea all over Billy.

"Oh, yuckers!" Billy wiped his face on his T-shirt.

He tasted Sarah's food. "This stuff is gross. No wonder she hates it."

Grandpa Stewie opened the refrigerator again. "How about something to drink? Your mother said her cup had juice in it."

"Yeah, okay." Billy left the bowl sitting on Sarah's tray.

He gave the plastic cup with the top on it to Sarah. She knew how to hold it in her fat hands. She tilted her head back and closed her eyes as she swallowed.

Billy took a deep breath. "That must be what she wanted."

He leaned back in the chair, watching his baby sister. She was okay, he thought. Not as great as a dog, but okay, sort of.

"Good work, son." His grandfather sat near Sarah's high chair.

"Thanks."

Sarah threw her cup on the floor. She smiled at Grandpa Stewie.

"Ba. Ba." She pointed to it.

Grandpa Stewie leaned over. As he was picking up the cup, Sarah grabbed a handful of mashed pea. She flung it across the room.

"No!" shouted Billy. A blob of mashed pea landed on Grandpa Stewie.

"Stop, Sarah!" Billy yelled. She threw another handful.

There was food all over Sarah's face, and all over Billy, too. The floor was covered with green plops.

"Mom's going to kill me!"

Grandpa Stewie burst out laughing. "This reminds me of when your mother was young. She did the same thing. All the time."

"My mother!" Billy couldn't believe it.

Grandpa Stewie chuckled. "She was the messiest of all the kids."

Billy wiped the floor. He tried to imagine his mother as a baby. Grandpa Stewie held Sarah while Billy cleaned off her high chair.

Billy washed Sarah's face with a cloth. She giggled and wrapped her hand around his finger. She tried to put it in her mouth.

"I think she's still hungry," Billy said.

"You know, I have this funny feeling she's teething."

Gently Billy put his finger into her mouth. He checked her gums the way he did the puppies at Dr. Mike's. "Hey, I feel a tooth!"

"Got a cracker or something she can suck on?"

Billy looked in the cabinets. "How about a chocolate-chip cookie?"

"Nope. It's got to be a biscuit or something hard."

Billy laughed. "I have dog biscuits."

"Give her one," Grandpa Stewie said.

"Really? You think it's okay?"

"I don't see why not. You eat them."

Billy handed Sarah a dog-bone-shaped biscuit. She put it in her mouth.

"She looks great." Billy laughed. "She's getting to be as good as a dog."

"Would you take her?" Grandpa Stewie asked. "My leg is starting to hurt."

Billy picked her up. "Good Sarah," he said. He brushed his lips against her hair. She smelled like a warm puppy.

There was a knock on the back door. "Hey, Billy. Can you come out?"

It was Howard. Billy paused for a moment. Then he walked to the door.

"No," he said through the screen. "You want to come in?"

Howard opened the door. He looked at Sarah. He looked at Billy.

"What are *you* doing?"

"Messing around with Sarah."

"Why?" Howard looked puzzled.

"'Cause I want to."

"You do?"

"Sure! You should have seen the mess she made before. It was great."

"What's she got in her mouth?"

"A dog biscuit. She's teething."

"She's eating dog biscuits! That's better than anything Frankie ever did."

"Yeah," said Billy. "I know."

Grandpa Stewie stood up slowly. "I think Sarah and I will take a little nap. Let's put her upstairs. Then you can go out, if you like."

"Great," Billy said.

9

A few minutes later Billy jumped off the back-porch steps. He ran across the grass and down the driveway.

"Wait up." Howard hurried after him.

Billy stopped and turned around. He still wasn't sure he wanted to be with Howard.

"Where you going?"

"Dr. Mike's."

"Can I come?"

"I guess," said Billy.

They took the route through the woods and came out on a busy street corner. They crossed with the lights.

"So what's been going on?" Howard pushed his sunglasses up on his nose.

"Nothing."

"Well, I went to the fair. They had great bumper-car rides. Made you sick as a dog."

Billy didn't say anything. He was thinking. Grandpa Stewie had said he had to speak up sometimes.

Billy stopped down the street from Dr. Mike's. He faced Howard. "Some friend you are."

"What are you talking about?" Howard took off his sunglasses and rubbed sweat off his nose.

"I got in trouble 'cause of you."

"What'd I do?"

"You said the garage-door opener was my idea. It wasn't. And you know it."

"I couldn't help it. My mother was yelling at me really a lot."

"Well, I lost my allowance on account of you."

"How come?"

"*Because* I have to help pay to fix your dumb door."

"What door?"

"The garage door, stupid head!"

"Well, it's not broken."

"What?"

"I came over to tell you. My father fixed it."

"Why didn't you say so?"

Howard shrugged. "I don't know."

"Yeah, well, I still got in trouble because of you."

Howard looked at the ground. He scratched the scab on his knee. "I'm sorry you got in trouble."

"Oh," Billy said quietly. Howard had never done that before.

Howard didn't look at Billy. "My parents make a big deal out of my telling lies. I didn't think you'd care."

"But I'm your best friend."

"I said I'm sorry."

"Okay," said Billy.

Howard looked up. "Really?"

"Yeah." Billy didn't know what to say after that, but he felt better. When they got to Dr. Mike's, he opened the gate. "Come on," he said. "I want to show you a neat dog." They raced over the field together.

The dogs were under the trees, hiding from

the late-afternoon sun. All of the different tails began to wag and thump as Billy and Howard came closer.

Billy dug out a couple of biscuits from his pocket and picked off the lint. He fed the pups and patted Lola. "I don't see him," Billy said. "Let's go inside. Dr. Mike must have him."

"Who?" Howard said, scratching the brown poodle's head.

"Come on, I'll show you."

But when they got to the back door, it was locked. They went to the front.

"They're closed Saturday afternoons," Howard said. He pointed to the sign in the window.

Billy pressed his face against the glass door. As hard as he tried, he couldn't see anything. He had a terrible feeling.

"Come on," Howard said. "Let's go. We can come back."

"No. I have to check something."

"What?"

"I have to see if my dog is there."

"You got a dog?"

"It was one of the strays. I wanted him."

"Oh," said Howard. He followed Billy around to the side of the building.

Howard let Billy stand on his shoulders. That way Billy could climb up on top of the toolshed. From there he looked into the room with the dog cages. The white dog wasn't there. "I can't believe it. Someone came for him."

Billy sat down on the roof of the shed. He wanted to cry. Over and over he said, "I can't believe it. I can't believe it."

"Come on," Howard said after a while. "I'll walk you home."

10

The kitchen was crowded when Billy got back home. His mother stood in front of the stove, frying chicken for dinner. Billy's father was taking ears of corn out of a steaming pot. Grandpa Stewie was putting place mats on the table. Nana kept trying to get mashed carrot into Sarah's mouth. Sarah only wanted to blow orange bubbles.

"Hi, Billy," said his mother. "You're just in time. Go wash up."

Billy didn't say anything. He just stood in the doorway.

"What's wrong, darling?" asked his grandmother.

Billy's voice shook. "Someone took my dog."

Suddenly there was silence in the kitchen. Everyone looked at him.

"What dog?" Mrs. Getten asked.

"There was this dog—" Billy stopped talking because tears stung his eyes. "I really liked him a lot."

"The white one." Grandpa Stewie put a hand on Billy's shoulder. "I was telling your parents about him."

Billy nodded.

Everyone was very quiet. No one seemed to know what to say.

Finally Grandpa put his arms around Billy and gave him a hug. "I think you should go wash up. Then we'll talk."

Billy made his way down the hall. Behind him he could hear his parents and grandparents speaking in whispers. He knew they were talking about him.

In the bathroom Billy sat on the edge of the tub. He rested his head on the sink. It felt cool against his face. Outside a car door slammed. A dog barked. Little kids yelled to one another. In the kitchen his parents were talking. Billy didn't want to move, he felt so sad.

"Billy," his mother called. "Food's getting cold."

Billy washed and dried his hands. He rubbed the tear stains off his face with a towel.

Everyone stopped talking when Billy came back into the kitchen. He sat down at the table.

"Grandpa told us about you feeding Sarah, Billy." His mother put an ear of corn on his plate.

Grandpa Stewie winked. "Yup. He saved the day."

"I'm really glad," his father said.

"Thanks," Billy said.

"And not only that," said Grandpa Stewie. "Dr. Mike told me Billy doesn't just teach her dogs tricks. He really helps her out over there."

"Good boy." Nana patted Billy's arm.

Billy just nodded. Nothing they said helped him feel better.

All of a sudden there was a loud bark. Everyone looked up.

"I guess we're not even going to get through dinner," his mother said.

There was another bark. Billy heard scratching on the basement door.

"There's one surprise that's busting its breeches." Mr. Getten smiled at Billy.

Billy stood up. He almost knocked his chair over.

"Go on," said Grandpa Stewie. "It's what you think."

Billy yanked open the basement door. "Oh, wow!"

The white dog leaped out. He jumped so high that his paws reached Billy's chest.

"Surprise! Happy birthday!" everyone shouted.

"But my birthday isn't until tomorrow!" Billy let the dog lick his face.

"There was no way we could have kept him quiet until tomorrow," Nana said.

Billy hugged and hugged the dog. "Thanks!"

They all moved away from the table and

stood around Billy. His father held Sarah so she could see.

"He's a beauty," said Nana.

"When did you get him?" asked Billy.

"This afternoon. When we were supposed to be at the mall."

"It's a good thing we didn't run into you at Dr. Mike's," his father said.

"Can I call Howard and tell him?"

"Sure," said his mother. "But wait until after dinner."

There were footsteps on the back porch. Then Dr. Mike opened the screen door. She held a sack of dog treats in her arms. "Hello! Did I miss the surprise?"

"No. You're just in time," said Grandpa Stewie.

"We were starting dinner, but the dog couldn't keep still," Billy's father said. He put Sarah back in her high chair.

"Sit down," said Mrs. Getten. "Let me introduce you to my parents."

"I've already met Grandpa Stewie." Dr. Mike smiled.

The family and Dr. Mike started dinner again. The dog settled down underneath Billy's chair.

Billy took a second piece of corn. Dishes

were passed around. The silverware clattered.

"What are you going to call him?" Dr. Mike asked.

"I don't know." Billy leaned over and slipped the dog a biscuit.

All of a sudden a little voice said, "Stew-ee."

"Did you hear that?" Billy's mother looked at the baby. "She said a real word."

"My name! I'm honored." Grandpa Stewie chuckled.

"Sarah," her father said. "Say, 'Daddy.' " He pointed to himself.

Sarah looked at her father. Then she leaned over the side of her high chair. She pointed to Billy's dog. "Stew-ee. Stew-ee," she said.

Billy looked at his sister and then at his dog. "You know what? I think Sarah just gave him a great name. Good Sarah!" Billy laughed. Then he slipped her a dog biscuit too.

ABOUT THE AUTHOR

When she was growing up, BETSY SACHS and her brother did pray for a dog but got a baby sister instead. They also had a cousin who ate dog biscuits. About *The Boy Who Ate Dog Biscuits*, Betsy Sachs says, "All I had to do was put the pieces together and I had a story." She lives in Waterbury, Connecticut.

ABOUT THE ILLUSTRATOR

MARGOT APPLE has illustrated dozens of books for children, including *Sheep in a Jeep*, her most recent picture book. She lives with her husband in the country outside Ashfield, Massachusetts, where she is always taking in stray cats. She now has five.